MOUSE
and
HIPPO

By Mike Twohy

A PAULA WISEMAN BOOK
SIMON & SCHUSTER BOOKS FOR YOUNG READERS
New York London Toronto Sydney New Delhi

For Evan

SIMON & SCHUSTER BOOKS FOR YOUNG READERS • An imprint of Simon & Schuster Children's Publishing Division • 1230 Avenue of the Americas, New York, New York 10020 • Copyright © 2017 by Mike Twohy • All rights reserved, including the right of reproduction in whole or in part in any form. • SIMON & SCHUSTER BOOKS FOR YOUNG READERS is a trademark of Simon & Schuster, Inc. • For information about special discounts for bulk purchases, please contact Simon & Schuster Special Sales at 1-866-506-1949 or business@simonandschuster.com. • The Simon & Schuster Speakers Bureau can bring authors to your live event. • For more information or to book an event, contact the Simon & Schuster Speakers Bureau at 1-866-248-3049 or visit our website at www.simonspeakers.com. • Book design by Alicia Mikles • The text for this book was set in Plumsky, Barbera, and Roger. • The illustrations for this book were rendered in India ink, water color, and felt pens. • Manufactured in China • 1116 SCP • First Edition • 10 9 8 7 6 5 4 3 2 1 • CIP data for this book is available from the Library of Congress. • ISBN 978-1-4814-5124-6 • ISBN 978-1-4814-5125-3 (eBook)

Oops,
excuse me,
I had an itch.

Your itch was me...
and... HELP...
I can't swim!

Would you like to open your eyes so you can watch yourself being rescued?

I'm sorry I dumped
you in the lake.

It really wasn't
your fault.
I should be more
careful where I
set up my easel.

Let me put your painting
back on the easel.

Wow!
This looks just like
real water!

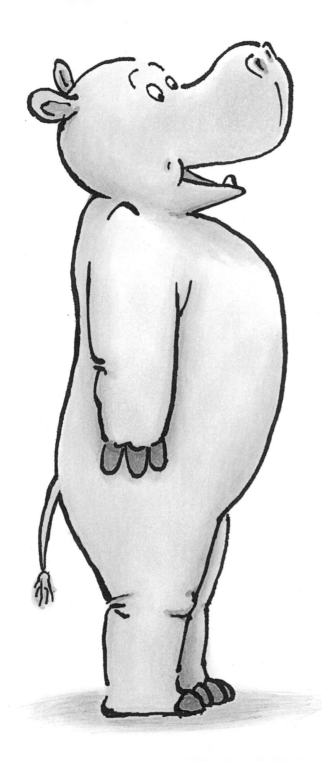

I want to look good.

Is this my best side?

Be sure to make me look
strong.

When I smile,
I have a little dimple.

I'm going to be quiet now.

As quiet as a mouse.

Gee—
you don't really
know how **big**
a hippo is
until you try to paint one!

There!
Done!

You can come look.

My paper
was too small
to fit all
of you in.

Do you like it?

It's **awesome!**

If I use my imagination, my ears are probably way up here—

and my dimple is right here!

I'm sorry.
Your dimple was higher
than my paper.

I can't wait to get it home and . . .

hang it over my bathtub.

You can come over
and see it anytime you want.

I love my portrait so much I'd like to paint one of you.

No one has ever
painted me
before either.
You can use my
paper and
my brushes.

You are so little
that I'm going to use
your littlest brush.

OK—stand still just like I did and be as quiet as a hippo.

It might help you to know that I like cheese.

And I'm a fast runner.

Also, my mother says I have beautiful whiskers.

You can decide where to cut.

There.

How does it look?

It's a little crooked.

That's perfect.

You can come over
and see it anytime
you want.